THE HERCULEAN OF BLOODSHED (ENGLISH)

THE RUMPUS OF ADOUR

SUMEET KUMAR

ISBN 979-888555147-2

Sumeet Kumar

Sumeet Kumar , A adult who experiences many phases of love in his life , get broked many times , stands up every time and keep moving to the next phases of the life.In reality he is a writter as well as singer (as a hobby).

Very exciting and interesting fact about him is that he is aauthor of New era i.e. he starts his journey of writing at the age when he was going to schools to get the study . His some famous works i.e. Maturity Of Love (Genre - Love),Privacy For Dream (Genre - Middle Class), Army Squad ofLove (Genre- The Seperation of Army Love), 5 Days of Love(Genre- Temporarily Love), Th e Endearment Of Love(Genre - Historical Era Of Love), Social Destruction Indo-Pak (Genre - The Story of The Love At The Time Of Division Of India And Pakistan), Middle Class Soul (Genre - The Dreams of Middle Class), The Accursed Kanatpur (Genre -The Horrific Story Of A Village), Wrong Number (Genre -The Suspenseful Physco Killer Story), The Secrecy OfDeadly Midnight (Genre - The Suspense About a Crime),Fragile Religious Of Death (Genre- The Death Of A TrustfulPerson), Nature Vs Science (Genre - The Future Battle Between Nature And Science In A Horrific Way), Generic Man (Genre - The Dream of I.I.T), The Unconsious 12 Hours(Genre - The Illusion At Stage Of Comma), The StrangeBurden (Genre - The Burden Of Love) , Her Existence (Genre- The Female Pain In The Society) , Jockstrap Prize (Genre -The True Story Of A National Athlete) , H Man [Hindi] (Genre - Superhero Tragic Story), H Man [English] (Genre - Superhero Tragic Story) , Maturity Of Love [Englsih] (Genre - Love) and many more are available on various geners on the offcial platform of **Amazon, Flipkart and Notionpress**. You can buy them from there.

Contents

Preface

Amy (The Main Character)

***Amy** is a student of nightmare Amre University. He is an orphan boy with no soul (The question How?? will be disclosed in a part of story). He is the **king of nipheria universe**.*

Stela (Main Character)

***Stela** is also a student of nightmare Amre University. He is an orphan boy* *with no soul (The question How?? will be disclosed in a part of story). He is the **king of darken world**.*

Hary

Hary** is also a student of nightmare Amre University. He is an orphan boy with no soul (The question How?? will* *be disclosed in a part of story). He is* ***knowledgeble about every Sword.

Alyona

***Alyona** is also a student of nightmare Amre University. She is an orphan girl with no soul (The question How?? will be disclosed in a part of story). She is the main **leader of the squad**.*

Giana

***Giana** is also a student of nightmare Amre University. She is an orphan girl with no soul (The question How?? will* *be disclosed in a part of story). She is an great **astrologist**.*

Tamun

***Tamun** is also a student of Nightmare Amre University. He is an orphan girl with no soul (The question How?? will be disclosed in a part of story). He contributes the main part of the story. He is the ruler **God of Bloodshed**.*

Acknowledgements

Aman Kumar

Special Thanks to **Aman Kumar** who worked so hard in the preparation of this book. He has continually put with my passive voice, omission of words, and late night calls. You have be en wonderful. Thanks to him for his precious time in reviewing proposals , individual chapters and early drafts, along with his suggestions on the applicability of the material to the world.

I

THE RISING OF EAST

In the world of God, every person is always associated with some journey or the other. Be on the right path and now if we follow our mother, then there is no one to stop us, in reality, peace is the desire of those paths where there is peace and if someone is found to accompany you in the happy journey, then victory in life is visible to heaven. It is known that there is always loneliness in the four walls and silence is also often seen and they say that if the walls of the house are silent, then happiness can never become your wish, this life always teaches us something unique, that's why We should never stop ourselves on any journey, enough should always keep moving forward, due to which we should never feel like dying while living And even if she happened to be with you by mistake, then maybe your grace has separated her from you, always the beginning of the journey. It is night, if someone has to move towards his destination, then first of all he should pursue his own thinking because the destination is easily visible, the paths that are there to walk on feet are probably difficult. In today's story The people who I am going to do the conversation never thought that we are in reality, even if we are in the world, it means that we are different from others. While achieving the goal, in front of the solitude of time, only his friends are saved, if he is not achieved at the right time, then everyone in the world has his own story, everyone's own journey is a destination. Whose feet I am going to tell you all, maybe they had never thought that there would be such a death in our life, even though people in the world are living in reality, their thinking always sees a statue dream only. It is exactly the same as adventure. Adventure is the word that people always use who are different from others and something different. There are many people who are successful in the world who are successful and if they leave the dream world and see their thinking in reality, then somewhere there is a desire for some adventure, only two things move in the life of a common man. It's a house and a house. Many people can also make it work. According to my life and my thinking, this is true to a large extent. If the morning of every day was the same, then a person would never progress in his field. The laughter of the moment everyone should try the curry of the day, not everyone is trying to make his life unbearable because he thinks every day that no trouble comes enough , today's day should be out in any way. His luck leaves him where he started his thinking, that is the fate of hard work, if the moon is always placed in the walls, then it remains safe, if it starts happening in a gathering filled with mistake, then it is your time. Right luck also started walking you on a wrong path, by walking on which you can neither rock yourself nor try to stop it.

"

There is no thinking
of hard work,
there is only luck,
and where there is luck,
there is no need to think in the gathering"

There are many animals in the world of animals who boast of their thinking feet and tell themselves better, they never get success with their feet, they probably do not know because nothing is permanent in the world, even our thinking is only a few. Time supports us and after a while, it also goes away from us. Pride is not a statue, it is a waste to become better, whose thinking is very different from us, if something is permanent in the world, then it is human rudeness. Those who always stay with him say why they have not sacrificed themselves, we never come alone in the world because we have our stubbornness to support us all the time. Their thinking is also given to someone and we have all been made by their thinking of the evidence they have given, when the human race was born in the world, then no one ever thought that humanity would divide the religion caste and a mystery was also a mystery. It is the knowledge which we insist on these days with the feelings of some kind, we never think that the reality in the world we are living in is the dream of some dream where trees Birds, humans and many types of animals, in the cycle line of time, for a time before birth to anyone, it was not thought that how much effort our ancestors would have spoken to their world, how many blood would have been shed, how many fears would have shed their anger. We must have burnt it, then we have to go somewhere else. It is said that no one can control the time stay feet we can walk with him and if we try to defeat his thinking then maybe it is also possible that he can also become the cause of our ruin because every crime in the world is the punishment for death and splendid foot too Whoever has rebelled against time till date, always has to face destruction instead of fate. Greed is also like a farg in today's world. We have not been able to remove our thinking from the illusion of love, so maybe the day is not too bad when the human race takes us inside the walls of the world. Will always be seen imprisoned and his care will also give up his fear like a mortal being He is immortal because his thinking always goes ahead for the sake of others I am not doing anyone's favor, I am placing the image of my thinking in the bash in front of all those who feel that God and the above have not given anything to us, it is everyone's fate is determined. There is infinity, we have always left our thinking and seen the statue of Pharaoh, in the world if a witness has more wealth than anyone, it does not mean that he is better than us and is far ahead of our thinking because he say no.

"Human beings even in a situation
why not to be hurt
why we keeps his thinking in us
in a sheet of poverty"

In the world of God, the statue of everyone is fixed, the feet of love are infinity, which we are aware of when we connect our own thinking with someone else's thinking and become slaves in his gathering, it is said that it is the voice of his own feet. Leaving the statue, his statue walks on his feet, the human race has become the key of only a difference in today's time, whose hope is Hans: We ask harm to someone in the world in which we are living, we ask harm to the animals of their own. At the end of the tax, we give them a sigh of relief, the loving feet we live in, we have not even left them, till today, where we see pollution, there are fights between Hindus and Muslims and everyone is only trying to change the khad and make themselves better than others. This thinking is not wrong, its image is wrong because if you have to change your own thinking, then change the world where your human birth race has started.

"when human change
the health condition
change
will go infinitely
if
you world
will change
then the whole

Creation
will go under a change"

Many people have come and many people have gone from the world and everyone's thinking meets each other at some point or the other, foot has anyone ever wondered why this happens undefined question The answer is also many, the answer is the same, everyone can also say that he is also human and we are also human, so our thinking meets each other, it is possible that by understanding the human race, the thinking of two people will meet. Is it right, is there a statue that proves it right? In the world, if a human's thinking meets another human's, then the only answer behind it is that their imagination of progress is the same. Their thinking meets each other. So a mother's love is never with him who is alive even in his worst condition, if someone has kept him alive even during the short time, then only mother's love is there if she is in the world if her love No, then there is no such love in the world of God that can support someone even in his bad condition.

"

The thread of breathe has stopped
but the wish of soul not
In the Identity of Time
the mirror is not clear for me now."

II

THE EVOULTION OF HUMAN

Human is a kind of son for the nature mother and the responsbilites of life circumstances ,there was no limitation of the humanity in this world because when we think about it ist gonna beyond our imagination and tthen it was classified the way of living character which was alive in our world earth ,so just look about the modern originated in africa within the past 200,000 years and evolved from the most likely recent common ancestor ,homo erectus ,which means upright man in latin .homo erectus is an extinct species of human life species of human that lived between 1.9 million and 135,000 years ago ,human evolution is the lenghtly process of change by which people originated from apelike ancestor .scientifc evidence shows that the physical and behavioral traits shared by all people originated from apelike ancestors and evolved over a period apporoxmiately six million years .there was always a question arises that did human evolve from apes ? no humans evolved alongside organutans ,chimpanzees bonobos ,and gorillas ,all of these share a common ancestor before about 7 million years ago ,and there was also consider the colour of the first human as a assumption as the history of human evolution ,humans probably had pale skin ,much like humans ,closest living relative ,the chimpanzee ,which is white under its fur ,around 1.2 million to 1.8 million years ago ,early homo sapiens evolved dark skin ,about 200,000 while ous ancestor have been around for about six million years ,the modern form of humans only evolved about 200,000 years ago . civilization as we know it is only about 6,000 years old ,and industrilization started in the earnest only in the 1800s,and the first humans emerged in africa around two million years ago ,long before the modern humans known as homo sapiens appeared on the same continent . around 430,000 ,the beanderthals have a long evoultionary history history ,the earliest known examples of neanderthal -like fossils are around 430,000 years old .the best known neanderthals lived between about 130,000 and 40,000 years ago ,after which all physical evidence of them vanishes ,this is excepted to occur between 1.5 and 4.5 billions years from now .a hig obliquity would probably result in dramatic changes in the climate and may destroys the planets habitability . most have been found in eastern africa ,in 2003 a skull dug up near a village eastern ethiopia was dated back to some 160,000 years ago ,its anatomical featurse -a relatively large brain thin-walled skull and flat forehead -made it the oldest modern human ever discovered . it is thus nicknamed the Eve Gene as it an inherited gene ,paying reference to the story of creation in genesis ,the first chapter of the bible the story of creation describes eve as first woman on earth ,there fore in essence she would be the mother to us all . 5 to 8 millions years ago ,shortly thereafter ,the species diverged into two seprate lineages one of these lineages ultimately evolved into gorillas and chimps ,and the other evolved into early human ancestors called hominids ,five stages of network evolution were identified exchange ,development expansion ,action and learning ,this integrative literature review points out the charcteristics of each of these stages also listing its constituent elements .

“

PREDICT
THE
FUTURE
REMIND
THE PAST
AND STAY
IN

THE
PRESENT
IS CALLED
THE
TIME
STABILITY."

The origin of modern humans has probably been the most debated issue in evolutionary biology over the last few decades.
Where did we come from?

"

"The exact origin of modern humans has long been a topic of debate.""

Our evolutionary history is written into our genome?. The human genome looks the way it does because of all the genetic changes that have affected our ancestors. The exact origin of modern humans has long been a topic of debate.

KEY FACT

Modern humans originated in Africa within the past 200,000 years and evolved from their most likely recent common ancestor, Homo erectus.

Modern humans (Homo sapiens), the species? that we are, means 'wise man' in Latin. Our species is the only surviving species of the genus Homo but where we came from has been a topic of much debate. Modern humans originated in Africa within the past 200,000 years and evolved from their most likely recent common ancestor, Homo erectus, which means 'upright man' in Latin. Homo erectus is an extinct species of human that lived between 1.9 million and 135,000 years ago.

Historically, two key models have been put forward to explain the evolution?(Adaptation based on the process of natural selection. Successful organisms survive and reproduce while unsuccessful ones die off.) of Homo sapiens. These are the 'out of Africa' model and the 'multi-regional' model. The 'out of Africa' model is currently the most widely accepted model. It proposes that Homo sapiens evolved in Africa before migrating across the world.

On the other hand, the 'multi-regional' model proposes that the evolution of Homo sapiens took place in a number of places over a long period of time. The intermingling of the various populations eventually led to the single Homo sapiens species we see today.

"Current genomic evidence supports a single 'out-of Africa' migration of modern humans.

This is still very much an area of active research, however, current genomic evidence supports a single 'out-of Africa' migration of modern humans rather than the 'multi-regional' model. Although, studies of the genomes? of the extinct hominids Neanderthals and Denisovans suggest that there was some mixing of genomes (1-3 per cent) with humans in Europe and Asia. This interbreeding between two previously separated populations is called 'admixture' and results in a mixing of genes? between the populations.

'Out of Africa': what's the evidence? ***'Mitochondrial Eve'***

There is more genetic diversity in Africa compared with the rest of the world put together.

Genetic studies tend to support the 'out of Africa' model. The highest levels of genetic variation? in humans are found in Africa. In fact there is more genetic diversity in Africa compared with the rest of the world put together. In addition, the origin of modern DNA? in the mitochondria (the 'powerhouses' of our cells) has been tracked back to just one African woman who lived between 50,000 and 500,000 years ago – 'Mitochondrial Eve'.

Our genomes are a combination of DNA from both our mother and father. However, mitochondrial DNA (mtDNA) comes solely from our mother. This is because the female egg contains large amounts of mitochondrial DNA, whereas the male sperm contains just a tiny amount. The sperm use their small amount of mitochondria to power their race to their egg before fertilisation. Once a sperm merges with an egg, all the sperm mitochondria are destroyed.

Your mitochondrial DNA is almost exactly the same as your mother's and her mother's.

As a result, mitochondrial DNA is described as being matrilineal (only the mother's side survives from generation to generation). So, your mitochondrial DNA is almost exactly the same as your mother's and her mother's.

Mitochondrial DNA has been extensively used by evolutionary biologists, as it is easier to extract than DNA found in the nucleus? and there are many copies to work with.

However, Mitochondrial Eve wasn't the first or only woman on Earth at that time. She was simply the point from which all modern generations of human appear to have grown. Evolutionary biologists think the most likely reason for this is that an evolutionary 'bottleneck' occurred during the time Eve was alive. This is when the majority of a species suddenly dies out, perhaps due to a sudden catastrophe, bringing it to the brink of extinction. If Mitochondrial Eve was one of the few women to survive then this could explain why her 'matrilineal' mitochondrial DNA ended up being passed along so many generations.

Similarly, DNA from the Y chromosome? is only passed on from fathers to sons and a evolutionary tree relating all present day male individuals also supports the 'out of Africa' model.

Further evidence for the 'out of Africa' model can be found in the size of human skulls. After studying the genetics and skull measurements of 53 human populations from around the world, scientists found that as you move further away from Africa, populations are less varied in their genetic makeup. This may be because human populations became smaller as they spread out from their original settlements in Africa and so genetic diversity within these populations was less. As a result the scientists stated that modern humans could not have emerged in different places, but instead had to have come from one region, Africa.

The oldest known remains of anatomically modern humans are the Omo I and Omo II skulls.

The oldest known remains of anatomically modern humans are the Omo I and Omo II skulls. These were found in 1967 in Omo National Park in south-western Ethiopia. The skulls have been dated to 195,000 years ago, highlighting how humans have evolved relatively recently.

Moving out of Africa

Evidence shows that the first wave of humans to move out of Africa did not have too much success on their travels.

At times it appears they were on the brink of extinction, dwindling to as few as 10,000.

The eruption of a super volcano, Mount Toba, in Sumatra 70,000 years ago may have led to a 'nuclear winter', followed by a 1,000-year ice age. This sort of event would have put immense pressure on humans. It may be that humans were only able to survive these extreme conditions through cooperating with each other. This may have led to the formation of close family groups or tribes and the development of some of the modern human behaviours we are familiar with today, such as cooperation.

"Genetically, the six billion people of today's world vary very little from the Homo sapiens that ventured out of Africa.

Between 80,000 and 50,000 years ago another wave of humans migrated out of Africa. These humans are likely to have been 'modern' in terms of their appearance and behaviour. Due to their newly cooperative behaviour they were more successful at surviving and covered the whole world in a relatively short period of time. As they migrated they would have encountered earlier, primitive humans, eventually replacing them. Genetically, the six billion people of today's world vary very little from these earlier Homo sapiens that ventured out of Africa.

Map showing human migration out of Africa.

A map showing human migration out of Africa. Image credit: Genome Research Limited

Admixture with extinct humans: what's the evidence?

Are Neanderthals our cousins or ancestors?

Homo neanderthalis, or Neanderthals as they are more often known, are an extinct species of human that was widely distributed in ice-age Europe and Western Asia between 250,000 and 28,000 years ago. They were characterised as having a receding forehead and prominent brow ridges. In 1856 the first Neanderthal fossil was discovered in the Neander Valley near Düsseldorf in Germany. Since then, researchers have been striving to uncover the position of Homo neanderthalis in modern human evolution. Homo neanderthalis appeared in Europe about 250,000 years ago and spread into the Near East and Central Asia. They disappeared from the fossil record about 28,000 years ago.

"Have Neanderthal genes contributed to the modern human genome?

Their disappearance has been put down to competition from modern humans, who expanded out of Africa at least 125,000 years ago (100,000-year-old remains of modern humans have been found in Israel), suggesting that there would have been a period of co-existence. Did the two species interbreed? Have Neanderthal genes therefore contributed to the modern human genome?

Initial studies of DNA from the mitochondria of Neanderthals showed that their mitochondrial DNA looks quite different to that of modern humans, suggesting that Homo neanderthalis and Homo sapiens did not interbreed.

Sequencing the Neanderthal genome

In 2010, scientists from Germany and the USA sequenced the DNA of an entire Neanderthal genome. They also identified another archaic human group called 'Denisovan', named after the Siberian cave in which the fossil finger, from which the DNA was obtained, was discovered. In 2013 they obtained a more refined Neanderthal genome sequence from a 50,000-year-old Neanderthal toe bone, found in the same cave in southern Siberia.

"The genome sequence suggested that early modern non-African humans interbred with their now extinct ancient human cousins.

DNA can survive in bone long after an animal dies. Over time the DNA from various microbes that encounter the skeleton will also invade the bone. As a result, the DNA can be contaminated with microbe DNA. Scientists therefore have to ensure that they sequence only the Neanderthal genome and get rid of any DNA material left behind by these microbes or resulting from contamination by modern humans who handle these bones. As with the human genome sequence, the Denisovan and Neanderthal genome sequences were made available online for free. The genome sequence suggested that early modern non-African humans interbred with their now extinct ancient human cousins as they journeyed along coastlines and over mountains.

Inbreeding is generally bad for the genetic fitness of a species as it reduces the variation in a population making it more susceptible to disease and illness.

Analysis of the Neanderthal genome revealed that the toe bone came from a woman as it had two X chromosomes. Further analysis showed that each pair of chromosomes was similar in sequence. This suggests that her parents were closely related, perhaps an uncle and a niece. Inbreeding is generally bad for the genetic fitness of a species as it reduces the variation in a population making it more susceptible to disease and illness. This reduced genetic variation could explain why Neanderthals became extinct.

When comparing human genomes to the Neanderthal genome, human genomes resemble each other more than any of them resemble the Neanderthal genome. Some

Neanderthal DNA is similar to DNA from people of European and Asian origin but these similarities are not seen in African DNA. This suggests that modern humans evolved in Africa and then expanded out into Asia and Europe, where Neanderthals lived. A degree of interbreeding between Neanderthals and early Homo sapiens then occurred in these areas. A study carried out in 2012 estimated that this interbreeding probably took place about 37,000-85,000 years ago and it is estimated that the proportion of Neanderthal-derived DNA in people outside Africa is 1.5-2.1 per cent.

From the past, to the future

FACTS :

Scientists have found nine Neanderthal genes in living humans known to be associated with susceptibility to conditions such as type 2 diabetes.

Nowadays, many of us carry a small fraction of DNA from our archaic Neanderthal and Denisovan ancestors. This shared DNA could have shaped our individual susceptibility to modern-day diseases or adaptation to new environments and climates. Scientists have found nine Neanderthal genes in living humans known to be associated with susceptibility to conditions such as type 2 diabetes, lupus and Crohn's disease. It has also been shown that high-altitude adaptation in Tibetans may be a consequence of archaic Denisovan DNA sequence in a region of DNA associated with haemoglobin concentration at high altitudes. Additional research is being carried out to investigate these links further.

For much of nature, natural selection and 'survival of the fittest' still play a dominant role; only the strongest can survive in the wild. As little as a few hundred years ago, the same was true for humans, but what about now?

What is a genome

A genome is an organism's complete set of genetic instructions. Each genome contains all of the information needed to build that organism and allow it to grow and develop.

In biology, evolution is the change in the characteristics of a species over several generations and relies on the process of natural selection.

Inheritance is the process by which genetic information is passed on from parent to child. This is why members of the same family tend to have similar characteristics.

Evolution of the human brain

The human brain, in all its staggering complexity, is the product of millions of years of evolution.

Genetic variation is a term used to describe the variation in the DNA sequence in each of our genomes. Genetic variation is what makes us all unique, whether in terms of hair colour, skin colour or even the shape of our faces.

Among evolutionary models that stress the Eurasian species, some consider Graecopithecus to be ancestral only to the human lineage, containing Australopithecus, Paranthropus, and Homo, whereas others entertain the possibility that Graecopithecus is close to the great-ape ancestry of Pan (chimpanzees and bonobos) and Gorilla as well. In the former model, Dryopithecus is ancestral to Pan and Gorilla. On the other hand, others would have Dryopithecus ancestral to Pan and Australopithecus on the way to Homo, with Graecopithecus ancestral to Gorilla. This morphology-based model mirrors results of some molecular studies, which show chimpanzees, bonobos, and humans to be more closely related to one another than any of them is to gorillas; orangutans (Pongo) are more distantly related.

III

THE TRAVELLERS

It is said that the journey in life gives us that happiness to an extent, where we forget ourselves and remember those moments, there should be no deserted right destination and there are not many other people who only say sati and somewhere they are also like you, then that life Looks like Paradise and paradise attach so there can only be known that one who says to live for himself says to live in those plains and climb those mountains where there are many more like us, the story I am about to begin In that too there were many such kind of travellers, who not only had their thoughts but also their habits, they used to love each other and we all are very aware of the thing that it is called friendship, no one ever thought that before coming into the world. Even more than blood relations, we will give importance to something in the world, which will be liked by our rudeness and we will name it as friendship with time. Such is the story of those six people who gave their whole life to each other. Wherever they went together, wherever they lived together, they never asked to be separated from each other because they considered each other as their life. Completing school together and doing college studies together after that, they were together all the time, in each other's happiness and sorrow, in every journey of life, even if someone was wrong in his happy time, even then he would never support each other. Never used to leave together, they say that to spend a good life, enough should be only a few moments, we lose it in the rivalry of time, do we have to bear sorrow for two moments, think about him all the time. Seeing the friends. these bottles are enough, I tell you all to take a journey on foot, where their relationship was not only of friendship but of blood, these bottles, the place where I am going to tell you the name of the country South Africa is where it was the beginning of all those who were about to become a superhero in the eyes of the world, they never knew these things about themselves because their parents themselves kept them away from their childhood. At a place where they were only six logs and no one I mean to say they did not have their parents with them, so let's make them all aware of you , (**ALYONA** , **HARY** , **STELLA** , **GIANNA** , **TAMUN** , **AMY).** These are the six witnesses who did not even know anything about themselves, neither their family nor their mother and father with them, nor any brother and sister. They were pale together since childhood. At the same time, they were living their lives by becoming each other's city, they were also very happy, I have already told this thing in the past, they all started their school and college studies together, but it was not just a school and neither In reality, in the eyes of the world, in the eyes of the world, it was only a dance, which was named after the name of "NIGHT AMRE UNIVERSITY" . That's why he was chosen by" NIGHT AMRE UNIVERSITY ", he was a witness in some way or the other, feet never told him about any thing, he used to work like a squad all the time, wherever trouble came, he came along. He used to wear legs everywhere all the time, he himself did not even know why he was doing it and how he was doing it because his fear was never in his own bash, he was not like anyone else. The rest used to walk, their thinking was never with them and there was one thing behind it too that even though their parents were not in the world, they never left their feet because they were born already born. conversation are also such that we can never trust the feet, we can see them, can feel them, can numb their candles, just like that their story was similar when those six mirror world feet came, only then their death is a happy day. Just like their parents, their anger had become their anger at the time and in their place their parents put their anger in the fear of their children, The head of night amre university was Miss Paul, who kept them all with her, gave them the love that their parents could not give them because they were not alive at that time, everyone wished that they had died by some cleric who There was a huntsman, an animal that had many surgical powers, and she killed them all while they were protecting their world. Like I was six, their parents were rotten super heroes, they were killed by SLAVATQ, Miss Paul never told them that their death was cash because they didn't say that their parents had turned away from them in their childhood. Even while fighting and escaping, she too should not get away from them, because even though she was only a head teacher for her parents, for Miss Paul, she was their child, she never felt her parents being an orphan. Let it happen because she never used to say that she should never be weak, that too because of his six friends. It was one of the most powerful towers in the world, that means, when their parents had a fight with their parents, they died with a single joint of the Born blade, how much and how true this thing is lie this only Miss Paul knew, Alyona was the head of her squad who was also the fastest and even at the forefront of the fight Miss Paul always told us the same thing, It was that Alyona you all are better and faster, Went to protect themselves, they never worked in war because at that time Alyona was the only one who was better than all of us, she always gave us our world, say that two four-eyed dragon fest why not .

DRAGON FEAST : 1500 BEFORE CHRIST

In a fight in which we were all injured, we were not able to know how to fight Dragon Feast for some time, because at the time we did not know anything about our own powers, nor did we upgrade at that time. It is a different matter that our training was done, we had never paid male legs and in that we were told how to face Dragon Feast, we were also told that no one paid attention to male legs at the time. Whenever we tried to kill Dragon Feast except Alyona, he used to take our way of society before we tried to injure him, Miss paul had explained it to us long ago in our training session. Even our own anger was not with us, because even though our fear was ours, when we came to know about our parents, when we came to know that we have been killed long ago and our anger has gone away from us long ago, then we This thing did not come to the society at this time that if we do not have any anger in our head and instead of our parents, then they have said Why didn't our female help us fight Dragon Feast because they had already fought with them, Dragon Feast first attacked Tamun's feet, after that we were all injured together. Legs Alyona had nothing to fold at the time. And we all wondered at the time that even after being so small, why nothing happened to it, why blood is not coming out of it like us because the she was special in our squad had fainted at the time which were green and tamun and lefts are injured leg left Alyona and I was very injured at some point, yet Alyona fought with him till the last moment and also gave him the last murder. Miss Paul told about Dragon Fest that he was the most beautiful of the savages. There is a special weapon, which was even more powerful than him, the foot Slavatq had taken control of him, because of which he is still his slave, Dragon Feast never die, only we can imprison him for some time. Legs they can never kill so how did Dragon Feast die on the same day was it a twilight, was it an illusion? How to Kill Dragon Feast On the way to death, he used to take out such a poison from his mouth, due to which our fearful feet used to get many types of shocks, we all had been hurt at the time, except Alyona, when we were all injured, Alyona said to all of us that Hole Come Back Nightmare.

Conversation

"***STELA** : But Alyona how do you handle this beast alone??*

***ALYONA** : I will take care of it Master Paul taught me to fight with it, you go and take the rest with you and keep it safe, I will come to the end of it.*

***STELA** : No we are a squad, we will fight together or we will die together.*

***ALYONA** : Its my order just go away .*

***STELA:** I'll leave them to safe and come to you again Alyona.*

***ALYONA** : No stella you have to go , "I LOVE YOU" .*"

After all I took the rest of Amy to the Niferia hole and left everyone to the nightmare where foot Miss Paul was already waiting for us and Amy left was injured so we're going to help Alyona again They were also nipheria hole through foot mirror bar where we both were supposed to go, we didn't even ask, I mean so pouched feet Amy was not with me, I was very scared at the time because when both of us were going to Alyona Then we both entered the Nipheria Hole at the same time. So Alyona had a pouch on her foot, that Amy wasn't her? Seeing her closer, she was very injured because when Dragon Feast attacked her legs with her eyes, she was very dangerous, due to which she was so injured that she was not able to even stiffen her feet. And when Dragon Feast last attacked him to die, it was time to save him, so I got Dragon Feast's sword in his place. I have never told one thing about T, he was not completely sharp, he had hands just like humans, Bucky's face was like a dragon and the name of his sword, Heeren Tont Thus, which is one of the most dangerous swords in the world. Seh was the one who was made into a piece of the universe, earlier this sword was also with the Slavatq, when the dragon Feast and the Slavatq hit you, then the Dragon Feast had hurt him, that too badly. It was given because he was the first warrior who did not feel hurt in front of Slavatq, just like our parents. It is said that if the sword of Dragon Feast strikes a person once, then he is sure to die, that too in a few moments. How can I live because I was only a human being, when his sword struck me, I had spoken in two parts, my parents' anger was separated from me and my fear was in Alyona's arms. So she could have avenged me, she didn't even survive the time, I told her before dying that Dragon Feast is very powerful. We can't defeat it, where even if it was for Alyona, my feet were finally in love, I don't know how I would let her die The one who was torn apart by an attack by Heeren Tont Only our squad knows it's only because Miss Paul died so I activated Alyona's code because of which Alyona went inside Nipheria hole without saying that and she went to that nightmare pouch, the lefts are already through That foot Amy didn't know anything about yet? And my death was probably at the time of her death, so Dragon Feast also lost her feet in a short time. At the time, my squad was feeling hopeful that I had died, was I really dead because how can a person who is born dead by his own birth be killed again? My squad's feet Miss Paul knew this, they never told me about everything, neither to Alyon nor to anyone else, that we can never die immortal, that too just like Dragon Feast.

"LOVE IS
THAT THING
IN WHICH
EVEN
DEATH ITSELF
SEEMS
A GIFT
THAT
TOO FOR ITS
SYMPATHIZERS."

I didn't know at the moment what world I had come to because it was dark everywhere but Miss Paul once mentioned that if the sword of Dragon Feast strikes someone with the Heren, we will never die. No feet are called in a world which is known as "Dark Rises" where our ancestors are also imprisoned. Behind it is someone else, it is like Dragon Fest and what will I get out of the dark recesses salt world How: How to save myself and come out to my Alyona How: Go who is my love I have to go to my squad also where How am I: come outside ? enough was asking himself a question at the time. I still had a question after all, is Amy okay, so why hasn't she returned to the Nightmare yet and that day has become invisible from the nipheria world.

"

THE LOVE
OF PAIN
WAS THERE
AND THE FEAR
OF DARKNESS

WAS ALSO
VERY
DIFFICULT
BECAUSE THERE
WAS NO LIFE IN
MY
PART TO LIVE
THAT TOO."

IV

THE WAR OF METERIODS

Some accidents happen like this in war too, about whom we do not know anything, we have no idea that what is going to happen with us in the future. Was injured, neither could I go back to my home because my parents' soul was not inside me, at the time whose Dragon Feast had imprisoned him for a long time And there was an attack which was done by Slavatq , that too with the help of meteroids, the meteroids were such a thing that even though the feet were like the shape of the stone, his thinking was always driven by the Slavatq , Miss Paul also talked about the meteroids in our training season. I had informed in which she had said that like the other killers of Slavatq , Meteroids are also a dangerous weapon among them, if with the help of this ,Slavatq will attack on our world, then our world will be divided into four parts, when our battle was fought with Dragon Feast, then Slavatq needed such a spirit that Because of this, he could wake up from his sleep, which was complete with my help, even without saying that because my body was in the dark world, my anger, my parents' soul near Dragon Feast and Dragon Feast of Slavatq . The most special weapon was my parents soul that's why Dragon Feast put my parents soul inside the Slavatq, due to which he woke up from his death after many years, our parents had very hard put his soul in Soul Prison World and to defeat him ,He had even given his life, because of my mistake, the whole world was in danger, even the univesrity could not do anything for him.

"IF I DIE
THEN MY
SOUL
WILL ALSO
TAKE
FOOT
IF THE SAME

ACCIDENT HAPPENED TO MY FAMILY THEN SHE WILL DIE ALIVE."

Soul Prison World was a place that was built by our parents and Miss Paul. there were many people whose name is still included in the book named "The Rivals of Dynamic ". when I first read this book, I Didn't even know whether it was true or all of it was written about our parents and Miss Paul and many of his friends that had created the world only to imprison for the evil spirits, in which the soul of the Slavatq was the strongest and Even the most dangerous, by which many people had even lost their lives in captivity. Now this accident was probably going to be our Nightmare's knee dance because my soul was now with the slavatq and what I feared was finally what happened this day After taking my soul. as he was freed from the prisoner, he first attacked our world with the help of meteroids and when he attacked then our world was divided into four parts in which many people of our members were touching each other , Were separated .by weak too and taking advantage of the weak time, Slavatq controlled everyone's soul one by one.

Hary and Tamun were also involved in it and the rest had no idea that they had finally come and said that when I was in the dark world, I could see everything at the feet of my world, because whenever I came out of it ,Trying to let go, a different right energy would make me go to her feet every time. one thing happened right in it that Amy returned to nipheria the whole world and the day he stepped back into our world, the day Slavatq attacked Amy and He also said to imprison her soul , there was a reason behind it, which Miss Paul had told while dying , that he tried to kill her soul . and as soon as he went to kill her he became invisible in a short time.

Conversation:

"

AMY : *I will kill you ! come in front of me" you impotent " just face my anger and my revenge .*
SLAVATQ : *Ha Ha , you are just a kid ,just grow up more to face my powers ,you are nothing in front of my powers, baby .*
AMY : If you want to see my powers then face me !
SLAVATQ : *Go away or else you too will die like your parents .(* ***I'M THE KING OF BLOOD*** *)*
SLAVATQ : *(laughing)........."*

After this, Miss Paul also came immediately and took Amy with her body. but she had also told to them that she didnt know that thing . but , really salvatq had kiiled our parents ? I think someone is included in these incident ?Will I be able to get my parents free again? Will everything be fine as before ? Will we ever find out our powers again ,after this and Miss Paul's if?

"JUST WAIT
FOR THE
SECRET KEYS

AND WAIT
FOR THE BIGGEST
WAR OF
FOUR DYANMIC
VILLAN .
"

The Unrevealed Part

The story will be continued in Edition II of this book. In the next part you will get to know about the great villians and the mystery of the main hero.

By: **Sumeet Kumar**

Rastar - Demon Level King

9 798885 551472

Printed by Libri Plureos GmbH in Hamburg, Germany